THE SHABBAT PUPPY

by Leslie Kimmelman illustrated by Jaime Zollars

MARSHALL CAVENDISH CHILDREN

In Hebrew, *shalom* has three meanings: hello, good-bye, and peace. *Mazel* (rhymes with "nozzle") means luck.

Marshall Cavendish Corporation
99 White Plains Road
Tarrytown, NY 10591
www.marshallcavendish.us/kids

Library of Congress Cataloging-in-Publication Data
Kimmelman, Leslie.
The Shabbat puppy / by Leslie Kimmelman ; illustrated by Jaime Zollars. — 1st Marshall Cavendish Shofar Books ed.
p. cm.
Summary: Every Saturday morning Noah and Grampa take a walk, looking for "Shabbat shalom"—Sabbath peace—but Grampa will not let Noah's noisy puppy Mazel come along.
ISBN 978-0-7614-6145-6 (hardcover) — ISBN 978-0-7614-6147-0 (ebook)
[1. Sabbath—Fiction. 2. Jews—Fiction. 3. Grandfathers—Fiction. 4. Walking—Fiction. 5. Dogs—Fiction.] I. Zollars, Jaime, ill. II. Title.
PZ7.K56493Sh 2012 [E]—dc23 2011016400

The illustrations are rendered in graphite and digital paint.
Book design by Vera Soki
Editor: Margery Cuyler
Printed in China (E)
First edition
1 3 5 6 4 2
Marshall Cavendish Children

For Margery C. and Natalie B.,
with much gratitude
—L.K.

For Griffin, who may not always
bring peace, but cannot help but
bring laughter and adventure
—J.Z.

EVERY SATURDAY MORNING,
Noah and Grampa take a Shabbat walk.

"It's the best time," Grampa explains, "to find Shabbat shalom, some Sabbath peace."

CAMP
SHALOM

And every Saturday morning, Noah asks if Mazel can come, too. “That wiggly, waggly, wet-nosed puppy?” says Grampa. He shakes his head. “He’s too noisy. How will I find Shabbat shalom if he’s along?”

Noah sighs. “How will we know when we find it?” he asks.

“You’ll know,” Grampa answers. “Shabbat shalom makes you feel good from the top of your head to the tips of your toes.”

One early Saturday morning, Noah and Grampa set out for the park. The sun is shining, the lake is sparkling, and Noah's shadow stretches out next to Grampa's.

“Look!” Noah says, as a butterfly flutters down and perches on top of his shoe. “Is that Shabbat shalom?”

“Sure is,” says Grampa. “And look at Mrs. Duck and her four ducklings out on the lake. That’s Shabbat shalom, too.”

"Mazel likes ducks," says Noah.
"Mazel would scare them away,"
says Grampa. "He doesn't
understand Shabbat shalom."

"Please, please, please," begs Noah on another Saturday. "Can't Mazel come today?"

"That bouncing, barking puppy?" says Grampa, raising his eyebrows. "He's still too noisy."

"Sorry, Mazel," says Noah, reaching down to pat him.

Noah and Grampa set out as usual. This time they walk through the woods behind Noah's house. The sun makes dancing dots of light on the trees, and colored leaves blow this way and that, like flying feathers.

"Mazel likes to chase the falling leaves," says Noah. "He's really funny."

“Hmm,” answers his grandfather.
“But not very peaceful.”

"Look!
Shabbat shalom!"
exclaims Noah, pointing to
a big spider web, glistening
with tiny droplets of dew.

"Shabbat shalom!" repeats Grampa,
pointing to a bush bright with
autumn raspberries.

He pops a berry into
Noah's mouth. "Sweet!"

When winter arrives, Noah says, “I promise Mazel will behave. Can’t we take him along this time?”

“That jumpy, jiggly dog?” asks Grampa. “He’s *still* too noisy for Shabbat shalom.”

Noah and Grampa set out again. As they step off the front porch, it begins to snow. They make a four-bootprint trail as they slip-slide along the sidewalks and blow puffs of cold air into the sky. "With Mazel along, we could have had an *eight*-footprint trail," Noah says, but Grampa just harrumphs.

“Look! Shabbat shalom!” exclaims Noah, holding out a mitten. Two perfect snowflakes have landed near his thumb. “Snowflakes are the best thing about snow. They’re magic.”

“I think the best thing about snow is the quiet,” says Grampa. “Shhh, listen.”

“I don’t hear anything,” Noah replies.

“Exactly,” Grampa agrees, squeezing his hand. “Shabbat shalom, Noah. Now how about some hot cocoa?”

Finally spring arrives. "You just *have* to let Mazel come today, Grampa," Noah says. "He's grown up a lot. He's quieter now."

Grampa looks at Mazel. “You know, maybe you’re right.” He reaches for the dog’s leash and winks. “Okay, you lucky dog. You’re coming with us.”

“Hooray!” shouts Noah. “Come on, Mazel!”

Noah and Grampa—
and *Mazel*—set out.

4212

In the park, Mazel stops beside a tree to smell. *Sniff, sniff.* He wags his tail. *Thwump thwump.* He starts to bark. *Yip yip yip!* Before Grampa can scold, "Quiet down, Mazel," Noah spies a baby bird hopping on the grass nearby.

"I don't think it can fly yet," whispers Noah.

Grampa nudges the fledging onto his newspaper, lifts it up, and gently tips it back into its nest.

“Awesome Shabbat shalom,” Noah says softly.

Grampa nods. “Awesome.” He leans down to give the dog a hug. Mazel’s tail wags madly.

“See? Mazel is the perfect Shabbat pet,” says Noah.

“Yep,” agrees Grampa. “You were right, Noah. Even a wiggly, jiggly, barking, bouncing dog can find Shabbat shalom.”

So now every Saturday morning, it's Grampa and Noah and Mazel who go for a walk. Always the three of them.

Shabbat shalom! Shalom, Mazel!